IN THE DOGHOUSE!

Written by
David J Robertson

Matador
9 Priory Business Park,
Wistow Road, Kibworth Beauchamp,
Leicestershire. LE8 0RX
Tel: 0116 279 2299
Email: books@troubador.co.uk
Web: www.troubador.co.uk/matador
Twitter: @matadorbooks

ISBN 978 1785893 223

British Library Cataloguing in Publication Data.
A catalogue record for this book is available from the British Library.

Printed and bound in Malta by Gutenberg Press Ltd.
Typeset in 13pt Gill Sans by Troubador Publishing Ltd, Leicester, UK

Matador is an imprint of Troubador Publishing Ltd

FOR MEGAN AND AMBER

SPECIAL THANKS TO MAZ AND HER RED PEN.

CHAPTER ONE

THE DEN

The three of us sat in Rascal's kennel.

Rascal's kennel is our den, although Rascal is too big for it now and won't fit inside. But for a Border collie like me, a small terrier like Bertie and a crazy spaniel like One-Eyed Rose it is just right.

We all fit in there perfectly, as snug as the bugs in a sausage-dog's rug, even with One-Eyed Rose's constant fidgeting. And that just goes to show how big Rascal is. He's enormous, even for a German shepherd. His thick black-brown fur makes him seem huge. I think that Rascal would seem very frightening to anyone who didn't know him. But those of us who are his friends know him only too well. The three of us can say without a doubt that Rascal is a great big scaredy cat – as cowardly as custard!

Rascal lay outside. Through the door of his kennel I could just make out his front paws, which are as big as my dinner bowl. His head rested on top of them as he dozed, his large black wet nose trembling as he snored softly. Occasionally he shook and whimpered in his sleep, probably dreaming that he was being chased – by a mouse!

'I'm bored,' One-Eyed Rose trod on my bushy tail as she paced impatiently about.

'Rose, will you keep still,' I shouted, 'or go outside and find something to do!'

One-Eyed Rose looked at me with her one good eye. She'd been run over by the school bus when she was a puppy and although the vet people fixed her up really good they couldn't mend her eye.

'Wow! That's a good idea, Misty, why didn't I think of that?' she pushed her way through the door, long floppy ears dragging along the ground, managing to tread on my tail again as she made her way out.

I sighed, raising my bushy brown eyebrows about to tell her off once more, but she was too excitable to take any notice so I went back to grooming myself. We Border collies are very fussy about our appearance and always make sure that our black and white fur is shown off as clean and sleek as can be.

Bertie sat at the back of our den stroking his long grey whiskers. He was probably thinking of good ideas. He has loads of good ideas. Bertie is very old and that means that he knows a lot of things about a lot of things. Bertie is a small terrier with short, wiry brown fur. He is always smartly dressed with a bone patterned scarf around his neck instead of a collar.

'She'll be back in a flash,' he said, nodding in the direction in which One-Eyed Rose had disappeared.

As soon as the were the words out of his mouth the spaniel rushed back. At the entrance she tripped over Rascal's paw, waking him up, before skidding through the doorway, treading on my tail and bashing into the back wall, just missing crashing into Bertie by the shortest of whiskers.

'Wow!' One-Eyed Rose sat up, 'It's started raining.'

CHAPTER TWO

BERTIE'S BIG IDEA

One-Eyed Rose was right. The rain started as a few miserable drops, but soon it was beating down on the roof of the den. The wind howled through the open doorway. But we were tucked up and comfy, our fur warm and dry.

Bertie was deep in thought.

One-Eyed Rose tried to nap, after all she couldn't sniff at this and sniff at that in the rain. Every time the gale blew particularly strongly she opened her one bleary eye and wrinkled her nose.

I watched through the open door as deep puddles formed and the water gushed in fast flowing streams toward the drains.

Something seemed wrong.

I tried to decide what was out of place.

I was comfy.

Bertie was thinking.

One-Eyed Rose was sleepy.

And Rascal was… Oh no, Rascal!!!

'Where's Rascal?' I shouted.

'What!?' One-Eyed Rose woke up with a start.

'What!?' Bertie stopped thinking his deep thoughts.

'Rascal! Where is he? He'll be getting soaked!'

We had to wait for the worst of the weather to calm down before we all set out to find our friend. It was still raining, but not as heavily as it had before. The wind still blew in gusts and it felt as cold as could be as we searched. One-Eyed Rose tried to sniff out where he had disappeared to, but the storm had been so fierce that it had wiped out any trace of the big shaggy dog. We decided to split up.

I went to look down the road. Bertie went to investigate up the road. One-Eyed Rose went to rummage in the neighbouring gardens trying to find our friend.

I looked under trees in case he was sheltering. I peered under cars to see whether or not he had taken cover. I barked to let him know that we were trying to find him. I could hear Bertie and One-Eyed Rose in the distance doing the same. We searched for ages.

Just as it seemed that Rascal had vanished I heard One-Eyed Rose frantically barking. She had found him! I scampered up the road following the noise.

Water ran from Rascal as he hung his head forlornly.

One-Eyed Rose had found him wedged between two wheelie bins, with an old magazine that someone had thrown out balanced on his head trying to keep dry. It hadn't worked. The magazine hat was a pulpy mess that squelched as we peeled it off. His fur was drenched and matted. He shivered, but with cold this time, not scarediness.

'I'm so sorry, Rascal,' I told him, 'we never thought that you couldn't find anywhere to stay dry.'

Bertie and One-Eyed Rose muttered in apology to our poor friend, ashamed that he had been so uncomfortable while we were all tucked up nice and warm and dry.

Steam rose in clouds from his fur. I was worried that he might catch a cold, or even worse, dog-flu! We had tried to dry him with the blankets from the den, but now they were soaked as well and our friend was a sorry, soggy sight.

'Shake yourself like this,' One-Eyed Rose tensed her tiny body, twisting first one way and then the other, spraying us all with the water from her own mottled grey fur.

'Rose,' I dribbled, 'you're wet too!'

'Wow! I forgot. Sorry Misty,' but the damp spaniel looked anything but sorry.

Fortunately for the rest of us, Rascal was feeling far too miserable to even try, so we escaped yet another soaking.

Bertie sat in the corner of our den, furiously stroking his long grey whiskers. I could tell that he was thinking – hard. 'I've had a big idea!' he finally announced.

'Wow!' shouted One-Eyed Rose, 'What is it?'

'We need to get Rascal a new kennel.'

CHAPTER THREE

THE KENNEL SHOP

'So where do we get a kennel from?' I asked.

'From a kennel shop, silly!' One-Eyed Rose answered.

'And where do we find one of those?' I looked at Bertie, hoping that he might be able to tell us.

Bertie shrugged, 'I don't know, I've never seen a kennel shop.'

Rascal sniffed and moaned, still shivering. A soggy puddle had now formed all around him and was growing bigger all the time.

'Well we need to find one quickly,' I said, 'we can't let poor Rascal suffer another cold and rainy day like today. He was very nearly drowned!'

Rascal spoke up forlornly in a croaky voice, 'Please don't go to any trouble on my behalf, I'll be fine.' He looked anything but fine and seemed very very sorry for himself.

'No that's not good enough,' I told him, 'we have to do something right away!'

One Eyed Rose said quietly, 'I know where there's a kennel shop.'

'What! Where?' Bertie and I chorused.

'It's over at the other side of town.'

'When did you go over to the other side of town?' asked Bertie, 'You never told us about that before.'

'I didn't like to. I was lost,' the spaniel said, 'you would have said that I was silly – again!'

'Were you sniffing at this and sniffing at that?' I asked her.

'Yes, not looking where I was going.' One-Eyed Rose admitted.

'As usual,' Bertie added.

'But I did find a kennel shop, come on I'll show you,' One-Eyed Rose shouted as she sprang to her paws.

Bertie held back, 'Wait, Rose – it's getting late. Perhaps we ought to leave it until tomorrow.'

'It won't take long,' One-Eyed Rose called over her shoulder. 'I remember exactly where it was.'

I looked at Rascal, still dripping wet. 'I don't that think we can wait,' I told Bertie, 'we need to find Rascal a new home now.'

It turned out that in a straight line the kennel shop wasn't far at all. Unfortunately the only way that One-Eyed Rose could remember how to get there was in crazy sniffing circles which let her sniff over here, sniff over there and double back to check out sniffy smells that she had nuzzled at before.

By the time we arrived it was getting dark. In fact the kennel shop wasn't a shop at all, it was a dirty, dusty yard surrounded by a high chain-link fence. There was a brick building at one end which was probably the office. It was in darkness. There was no sign of life. But One-Eyed Rose had been right. Inside there seemed to be kennels of every description and they all seemed to be very big. Very big indeed!

I pushed at the gates,

but they were bolted from the inside. 'It's closed!' I shook my head sadly, 'Now we'll have to come back tomorrow after all.'

'Never mind,' said Rascal, 'with all that walking I've nearly dried out now.'

'Tomorrow it is then,' said Bertie. Then as he looked around, 'Where's Rose?'

CHAPTER FOUR

THE FLYING KENNEL

'Perhaps she's gone home already,' Rascal muttered. 'We ought to go back and find her,' he turned back the way we'd come, glad of an excuse to leave before we got into trouble.

'I don't think she's gone anywhere!' Bertie pointed a paw into the compound.

One-Eyed Rose scurried past, sniffing at this and sniffing at that. She didn't notice the three of us standing just outside.

'Rose!' I shouted, 'How did you get in there?'

One Eyed Rose stopped sniffing and looked up. 'Oh! Hi guys. I found a hole in the fence,' she nodded behind her.

'Well you'd better come out quickly,' Rascal blustered, 'before we all get into trouble!'

Bertie stroked his long grey whiskers, 'It might not hurt to take a quick look. If there's nothing suitable for Rascal's kennel then we won't need to come back tomorrow.'

'Oh-oh!' Rascal sighed, 'that sounds like another one of those adventures is about to happen.'

'I think that Bertie's right, after all what harm can it do?' I asked him, but Rascal just shuddered.

We made our way around the fence line until we came to the hole that One-Eyed Rose had told us about. It was enormous. A lorry was parked at the side of it, loaded up with lots of the big kennels. It looked as if there was only room to get one more on.

'Something's not right,' Bertie examined the fence. He sat and stroked his long grey whiskers deep in thought. 'I think that someone has cut through here on purpose!'

'Oh, oh! Time to go!' Rascal would have run away if I hadn't been standing in his way.

'We can't go without One-Eyed Rose,' I told him.

Rascal muttered under his breath something about little dogs always getting him into big trouble as I pushed him through the hole.

Bertie followed, sniffing the ground to track our silly friend's scent. 'Come on, she went this way.'

One Eyed Rose sat in the middle of the compound next to a sign that had the words,

written in big bold letters. 'Wow! I wonder what this notice says? These kennels are ever so big,' she told us as we approached, 'They're all perfect for our new den.'

'Rose is right. They're ideal. What do you think?' I asked Rascal.

'I think we ought to go and come back tomorrow when the kennel shop is open properly.' Rascal whispered.

One-Eyed Rose bumped the door to the nearest wooden shack and it swung open. She darted inside. 'It's really roomy. We could all fit in here easily. Even with Rascal!'

Bertie peered through the entrance, 'Rose is right. We would all fit in here just as snuggly as snug could be.'

'Let's not forget that it's supposed to be Rascal's home.' I told them. 'Rascal needs to feel happy in there.'

'Of course,' Bertie sounded a bit embarrassed, I think he had forgotten that we were supposed to be finding our friend a house.

One-Eyed Rose wasn't so easily distracted though. 'Look at this one! Wow! It's even got a balcony,' shouted the excited spaniel, who had now moved on to a kennel with another sign that we couldn't read,

hanging from the roof. 'It's got windows and everything, we could have some great parties here!'

In the distance something made a whirring sound.

'Ssh, Rose,' hissed Bertie. 'I can hear something!'

Rascal trembled.

Bertie stroked his long grey whiskers.

I looked around anxiously.

One-Eyed Rose and the kennel slowly lifted into the air and floated across the ground.

CHAPTER FIVE

AAARGH!

Rascal dropped flat to the floor and covered his eyes with his front paws, terrified as usual, unable to make sense of what he could plainly see. The kennel was flying! As it went higher One-Eyed Rose leaned on the balcony rail and peered over the edge.

Bertie looked at me.

I looked at Bertie.

We both turned to watch as One-Eyed Rose and the kennel hovered in the air. The spaniel now scampered around the balcony, 'Wheeee!… I'm flying. Wow! This is great!'

Slowly the kennel turned and we could see that it had been picked up by a big yellow fork lift truck. A chubby man with red cheeks was driving. As we saw him, he saw us.

'How did you dogs get in here? Scoot! Go on, get lost!' he seemed very angry as he waved his arms, shooing us away.

Rascal needed no encouragement. He leapt to his paws and shot off across the yard, obviously looking for somewhere to hide.

The driver watched him go, 'Goodness, he was big!' he muttered. His hands grabbed the steering wheel again, but it was too late – the truck was out of control!

It spun around to the left.

One-Eyed Rose slid across the balcony.

The truck spun around to the right.

One-Eyed Rose slid back again.

The man shouted in fear.

I barked in alarm.

Bertie groaned. 'Oh no!'

One-Eyed Rose laughed, 'Wheeee!'

Another man, a lot thinner than the first, appeared from inside the office to see what the commotion was. 'What's going on?' he shouted, as the fork lift truck hurtled toward him. His eyes opened as big as saucers as he realised what was happening, his hands reaching up to cover his bald head, as if that would stop him from getting squashed. He looked as scared as Rascal.

The driver shouted, 'Get out of the way!' as he jammed on the brakes.

The fork lift skidded.

The thin man turned and ran, mouth open in a silent scream, arms now waving in front of him.

Tyres squealed.

The whole truck tipped forward.

The big kennel slid off the forks and bounced along the ground.

One-Eyed Rose was thrown high into the air.

The balcony broke away and kept on going.

The kennel dug itself into the ground, wood splintering as it stopped. Luckily most of the glass in the windows was still in one piece, although the door was hanging from broken hinges.

One-Eyed Rose dropped out of the sky and into the thin man's outstretched arms as he was still running.

'Oh! Hello, my name is Rose, so very nice to make your acquaintance,' our friend politely introduced herself in her poshest voice, 'and tell me, whom do I have the pleasure of landing on?'

'Aaargh!' not understanding what the spaniel was barking about, Baldy tossed her back into the air, ran into the office and slammed the door shut behind him.

One-Eyed Rose cartwheeled gracefully across the yard and dropped on all fours into the balcony once more as it came to a gentle stop. 'Wow! Was it something I said?' she asked, as she calmly dusted herself off.

CHAPTER SIX

WHERE'S RASCAL?

On the fork lift truck, the man rested his head on the steering wheel. His shoulders bounced up and down, I think he was crying.

One-Eyed Rose licked her messed up fur back into place. I looked at the wreckage and Bertie sat stroking his long grey whiskers. 'I think we're in trouble,' he said.

The office door creaked open and the thin man peered around it.

He looked at the balcony.

He looked at the broken kennel.

He glared at Bertie.

He scowled at One-Eyed Rose.

He crossed the yard quickly and aimed a kick at me, 'Get out!' Fortunately he was too far away to make contact.

'That's not very nice!' I barked at him.

'Don't you hurt my friend,' yapped Bertie, 'we're going.'

One-Eyed Rose joined in, 'We don't want your rotten kennel anyway – it's broken!'

'Come on, Rose,' I hissed.

'But if it's alright with you we might come back tomorrow and look at one that's in one piece,' she carried on as I pulled her away.

We ran back through the hole in the fence. The door to the lorry was open, so we jumped into the cab to hide. It didn't seem as though either of the men had chased us, they must have been far too busy. Eventually I picked up the courage to peer over the steering wheel. There was no one in sight and in the yard I could hear the fork lift truck driving about once more.

'We're safe!' I sighed.

'Good!' Bertie puffed out his cheeks in relief.

A terrible thought struck me, 'Oh no! We've left Rascal in there!'

Bertie stroked his long grey whiskers, 'We'll have to go back in there and find him before that nasty man does.'

'This might help if we get caught,' One-Eyed Rose told us. She had been studying the controls of the truck. 'They've left the keys in here, anyone could steal this lorry.' She pulled out the keys with her mouth. 'I'be tell vem wig stogged thap frog haffening,' she muttered with a mouth full of metal.

'What did she say?' I asked Bertie.

He shrugged, 'I think she's trying to say that she took the keys to stop the lorry from being stolen, so that we can get into their good books.'

The three of us snuck back into the yard. At least One-Eyed Rose was quiet for a change – her mouth was still full of keys. Somewhere amongst all the kennels we heard the sound of voices and the fork lift truck working away.

'Where's Rascal?' I whispered to Bertie.

'I don't know,' Bertie admitted.

One-Eyed Rose nodded toward the office, 'mmph, mmph,' she mmphed, as she scampered off in that direction.

We followed and sure enough, hiding behind the building, lying on the ground with his front paws over his eyes as usual and his trembling bottom stuck up in the air was Rascal.

'Rascal, come with us, quickly, you can't stay here.' I hissed.

'Noo!' moaned Rascal, 'It's too far to run back over to the fence. We'll get caught by that angry man. He'll shout at us again!'

'He's got a point,' muttered Bertie. 'Listen! It sounds as if they're coming back.'

I cocked an ear. The truck noise was getting louder.

'Mmph,' One-Eyed Rose nodded toward the gate. It was much closer than the hole in the fence, but it was closed.

Bertie stroked his long grey whiskers, thinking furiously. 'Rascal!' he shouted, not even having time to announce that he'd had a big idea. 'Get up! If you can get to the gate you're big enough to open the latch with your teeth and then we can all escape.'

Rascal lifted a paw from his eyes and peered at the gate. 'Oooh!'

'Oi!' It was the thin man. He must have heard Bertie. 'You dogs! I thought I told you to clear off!' He made as if to run toward us.

That was enough to spur Rascal into action, he didn't want to get caught.

He stood up, towering above the rest of us dogs.

The thin man saw him, 'Oh my! Where did that great big wolf come from?'

Frightened by the man, Rascal ran for the gate.

The man ran in the opposite direction, terrified of Rascal.

The fork lift truck rounded the corner with another big kennel on the front. Seeing Rascal in full flight the driver leapt from his seat and followed his friend, screaming loudly, 'Aaaaargh!'

The uncontrolled machine kept on going, speedily careering round in circles.

CHAPTER SEVEN

MR. CHIEF INSPECTOR

Rascal reached the gate.

The men reached the fence.

Rascal twisted the latch and pulled the gate open.

WA WA WA WA. The alarm went off!

The thin man jumped into the lorry.

'Mee's,' One-Eyed Rose shouted as best as she could with a mouth full of keys, 'By'b dot yous mee's.' She hurtled off toward the men.

Bertie sat watching the commotion. 'What is she telling them now?' he asked me.

The fat man looked over his shoulder and saw her coming. He screamed. She looked fierce with only one good eye, like a crazy pirate dog. 'She's only trying to say that she's got your keys,' I barked loudly after him. That seemed to frighten him even more.

WA WA WA WA! The alarm kept going.

The fork lift truck crashed into the first kennel, buckling the walls as it stopped.

One-Eyed Rose vaulted over the wreckage.

The fat man jumped on top of the thin man in the driver's seat.

The new kennel teetered on the end of the forks.

WA WA WA WA!

Rascal had turned and was running away from the scary alarm.

Another noise began in the distance. *NE NA, NE NA, NE NA.*

The new kennel swayed over the old one.

The thin man pushed the fat one out of the truck, 'Gerrroff!'

WA WA WA WA!

NE NA NE NA NE NA! The second noise got louder.

I looked at Bertie, he was staring wide eyed at the fork lift truck.

The kennel on the forks swayed forward.

It seemed to move in slow motion.

It tilted back again.

Creaking on the forks it pitched over one final time.

RAAARK!

It fell with an almighty *CRAAASSSH!*

The windows on the first kennel exploded outwards.

The door fell off altogether.

The buckled walls burst and flew apart as the roof caved in.

Rascal overtook One-Eyed Rose in terror and tore through the fence.

The fat man tumbled to the ground.

'Where are the keys!?' yelled the thin man.

NE NA NE NA NE NA! Something was coming toward us, very fast indeed!

A white car with a red stripe and flashing blue lights slewed around the corner and screeched to a stop.

WA WA WA WA! The alarm must have alerted the police.

Rascal couldn't get past the lorry and the fat man. He stopped and smiled as best as he could, certain that he was in big trouble, 'Ever so sorry!' he said, 'But I think you might find that none of this was my fault!'

A policeman leapt from his squad car. He saw Rascal who seemed to be growling and baring his teeth at the terrified fat man.

One-Eyed Rose shot through the fence and dropped the keys at the policeman's feet. 'I only took these to stop anyone from stealing these poor men's lorry,' she told him, 'please don't send me to prison!'

'What on earth is going on here?' asked the policeman. 'And what are you barking about?' he looked down at One-Eyed Rose.

WA WA WA WA!

'Come on!' I told Bertie, 'we'd better see if we can help our friends.' We dashed off to catch up to the action.

NE NA NE NA NE NA! Another siren added to the confusion.

A second policeman's car sped up and stopped alongside the first. 'What's going on here, constable?' asked the policeman who got out. He was wearing a very smart uniform with a lot of shiny medals on his chest.

'I'm not sure, sir,' said the constable, 'but I think that this burglar was stealing sheds and summerhouses.'

Neither of them noticed the thin man who had slithered out of the lorry and was trying to tiptoe away.

I dashed through the fence.

The burglar was looking over his shoulder to see what the policemen were doing. He didn't see me.

I ran into him and accidentally tripped him up.

He fell and sat hard on his bottom. *WA WA WA WA!*

Bertie followed me through the fence, bumped into the burglar as he was trying to get up and knocked him flat on his back.

Dizzily I stumbled over Bertie and sprawled onto the burglar's chest, pinning him to the ground. 'Oops! Sorry!' I barked at him. 'I do beg your pardon.'

CHAPTER EIGHT

THE NEW DEN

'So,' said the constable, pointing at Rascal. 'It seems that this dog foiled the burglary, Mr. Chief Inspector sir. He must be very brave indeed.'

Mr. Chief Inspector looked at Rascal and shuddered. 'My, my. He does look fierce. I wonder if he would like to be a policeman's dog?'

'I don't think so,' Rascal trembled and whimpered at Mr. Chief Inspector, 'if that's alright with you?'

'I don't think that the uniform would suit him!' One-Eyed Rose told the policemen.

The two naughty burglars were in handcuffs looking on. They didn't look very happy at all.

The constable gently stroked One-Eyed Rose. 'It seems that this nice little dog took the lorry keys so that these nasty villains couldn't get away.'

Mr. Chief Inspector patted me on the head. I think that he might have patted Bertie as well, but Bertie is only small and he couldn't reach without bending down. 'And I watched as these two caught the other baddy,' he said, 'they both tripped him up and pinned him to the floor. Perhaps we should give them a medal.'

'I don't know what a medal is,' I told Mr. Chief Inspector, 'but we would much prefer a new kennel.' I ran over to the wreckage and began to bark at it so that they might understand what it was that I wanted.'

Bertie, One-Eyed Rose and Rascal all ran over to me and began to bark too.

'Hmm, I wonder?' Mr. Chief Inspector said, stroking his chin.

The constable stood back and admired his handiwork. Both of the broken summerhouses had been delivered to Rascal's and the policeman and Mr. Chief Inspector had worked really hard to repair them. Eventually they had managed to make one good one out of the pieces.

The door creaked as it opened, but that was fine. At least we could close it if the weather got nasty – again.

The windows were nailed shut and repaired with wooden boards instead of glass. But that meant that we didn't need curtains when it was dark.

The roof was patched, but it didn't look as though it might leak, so at least we would all be dry.

The walls were also patched up and newly painted. They would stop any nasty draughts if the wind blew.

The balcony had been fixed back on and now we would have somewhere to sit in the sun when the day was nice.

'Good job, constable,' said Mr. Chief Inspector. He turned to look at me and my friends as we sat watching. 'I hope that you enjoy this summerhouse. It is a fitting reward for your help in catching those criminals.'

'Wow! What nice policemen. What's a summerhouse?' asked One-Eyed Rose.

Bertie stroked his long grey whiskers, 'It must be another word for a big kennel.'

We watched as they drove away with our old den strapped onto the back of the lorry.

'I had some good big ideas in there, I shall miss it,' said Bertie. He sounded a bit upset.

'Wow – there were some great sniffy bits in our old den, I shall miss it too,' said One-Eyed Rose,' snuffling back a tear.

'We had some good old times,' I said with a lump in my throat.

'Well I could never fit in it, so I won't miss it at all!' said Rascal happily as he wandered into his new kennel to have a lie down and a well-deserved rest.

One-Eyed Rose began to scurry about in circles, sniffing at this and sniffing at that. Perhaps this new den might not be so bad after all.

Bertie and I sat on the patched up balcony as the sun poked out from behind the clouds. It was getting warmer and I was feeling very tired after the excitement of the night before.

'It looks like it might be a nice day,' muttered Bertie.

'A very nice day indeed!' I agreed, gently laying my head on my front paws and closing my eyes.

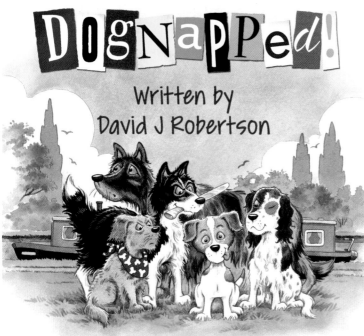

DogNaPPed!

Written by
David J Robertson

Illustrated by Ian R Ward

HAVE YOU READ THE STORY OF MISTY AND HER FRIENDS ADVENTURE ON THE CANAL?

PROUD TO BE A FINALIST IN THE PEOPLE'S BOOK PRIZE 2017

Cast accidentally adrift on a canal boat with the boat's reluctant puppy, Ashley, four doggy friends find themselves in BIG trouble.

"News is coming of a dognapping! Young Ashley has been taken along with a narrowboat. His people are very upset. In a statement they said, "Whoever has taken our poor puppy is very naughty indeed'."

Can Misty, Bertie, Rascal and One-Eyed Rose prove their innocence? Can they even make it safely back to shore? Can any of them swim? Whatever happens, it will be an adventure to remember!

WHAT SOME ACE REVIEWERS HAVE SAID ABOUT

DOGNaPPed!

FINALIST IN THE PEOPLE'S BOOK PRIZE 2017

I enjoy adventure books and this one is number one of all of them. The one character I like the best is Misty because I got a dog called Misty too.

Macey Cullen - age 8 class: 3

I think the book was really good. There were lots of funny bits and some exciting bits too.

Niamh Walker - age 10

I think it's funny and very adventurous. There are lots of adjectives. It includes lots of different types of animals.

Brena Cadman - age 10

DOGNAPPED! is funny, I really loved Misty and the other dogs in this story and the missing puppy Ashley was very sweet too. The pictures are lovely because they are very colourful and pretty.

Annable John-Ligali age 5 1/2 - Books and Authors U.K. (This book was read as a bedtime story by Annabel's mum, Anne - also from Books and Authors U.K. who wrote: There are children's stories which are exceptionally awesome and you want to read them again and again. DOGNAPPED! is a book that falls into that category).

COMING SOON

THE LATEST MISTY ADVENTURE –

ON THE DOG WALK!

www.mistybooks.net